High, Wide & Handsome

& THEIR

Three Tall Tales

HANDSOME

AND THEIR
Three Tall Tales

by Jean Merrill & Ronni Solbert

Young Scott Books

Library of Congress Card Catalog No. 64-13584

TEXT © MCMLXIV BY JEAN MERRILL. ILLUSTRATIONS © MCMLXIV BY
RONNI SOLBERT. ALL RIGHTS RESERVED. MADE IN U.S.A.

FOR

Christopher Solbert

IN A VILLAGE on the road to Pegu, there lived three friends: High, a monkey; Wide, a pig; and Handsome, a fox.

High, Wide and Handsome were the laziest

fellows in the countryside. While everyone
else was working very hard, they lay on the
veranda of the village rest house, telling stories
and drinking palm toddy.

High, Wide and Handsome liked to hang
around the rest house, because there was al-
ways the chance that a traveler would treat
them to a palm toddy or a nice dinner in
return for a story.

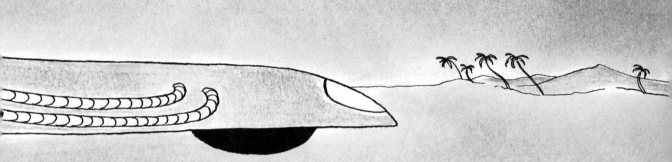

One day a hound drove up to the rest house. His name was Rolling Stone. Rolling Stone had a yellow sports car and was dressed in the most beautiful clothes that High, Wide and Handsome had ever seen.

Rolling Stone's jacket was embroidered, his trousers were brocaded, his walking stick was jeweled, his hat was feathered, and his red velvet slippers turned up at the toes.

High, Wide and Handsome stared at the splendid stranger.

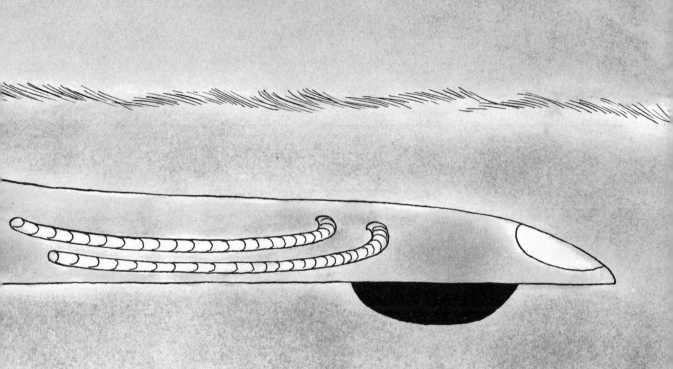

"Oh, those slippers!" sighed High.

"Oh, those trousers!" sighed Wide.

"That feathered hat and that walking stick!" said Handsome.

The clothes that High, Wide and Handsome wore looked very ordinary beside Rolling Stone's.

High, Wide and Handsome tiptoed around Rolling Stone as he sipped a palm toddy on the veranda.

High whispered to Wide, "Do you think we can get him to treat us to a nice lunch?"

"I have a better idea," said Handsome. "Let us trick him into giving us his beautiful clothes."

"How?" said Wide.

Handsome whispered his plan to his friends, and they agreed that it was a very good plan.

So when Rolling Stone had finished his toddy and was ready to travel on, Handsome pranced up to him and said, "Why travel in the heat of the day? Stay and have lunch with me and my friends."

"Why, thank you very much," said Rolling Stone. "I will."

High, Wide and Handsome treated Rolling Stone to a fine lunch. Then, after lunch, everyone stretched out on the veranda to rest.

While they were resting, Handsome said, "Let us make a bet to see who can tell the most unusual story."

"All right," said Rolling Stone. "But how shall we judge which is the most unusual story?"

"The story must be so unusual," High said, "that someone says, 'I don't believe it!'"

"You mean that if I tell a story so unusual that you do not believe it, I will win the bet?" asked Rolling Stone.

"That's right," said Wide.

"And will there be a prize for the winner?" asked Rolling Stone.

"Of course," said Handsome. "Whoever loses must become the slave of the winner and do whatever the winner orders him to do."

"That is a bet worth winning," said Rolling Stone.

High, Wide and Handsome smiled to themselves. They were certain that one of the stories they were going to tell would be so astonishing that Rolling Stone would forget himself and exclaim, "I don't believe it!" Then he would be their slave, and they would order him to give them his clothes.

"Would you care to begin?" High asked Rolling Stone.

"No, I shall have to think," said Rolling Stone.

"Then I will begin," said High.

Already High could see himself dancing down the road in Rolling Stone's velvet slippers. With his eye on the slippers, High began to tell his story:

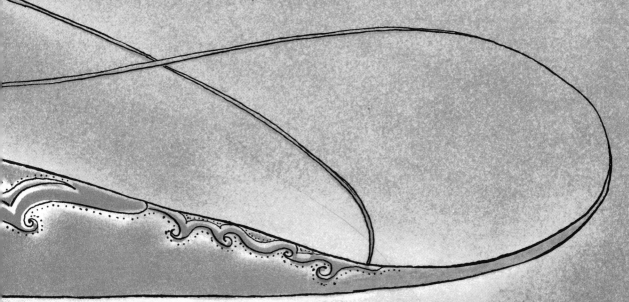

High's Story

"Last week," said High, "I got in my boat and went fishing. I was having very bad luck, and I asked some other fishermen how they were doing.

"They told me that they had not caught anything, either. So I decided to see what was going on at the bottom of the river. I dived into the water, and it was three days before I touched bottom.

"When I got there, I discovered that
a fish as big as a mountain was eating
up all the other fish.

"I killed this monster fish with one blow.

"Then, as I was hungry, I built a fire and roasted the monster and ate him at one sitting.

"After that I floated back to the sur-
face, got in my boat, and came home."

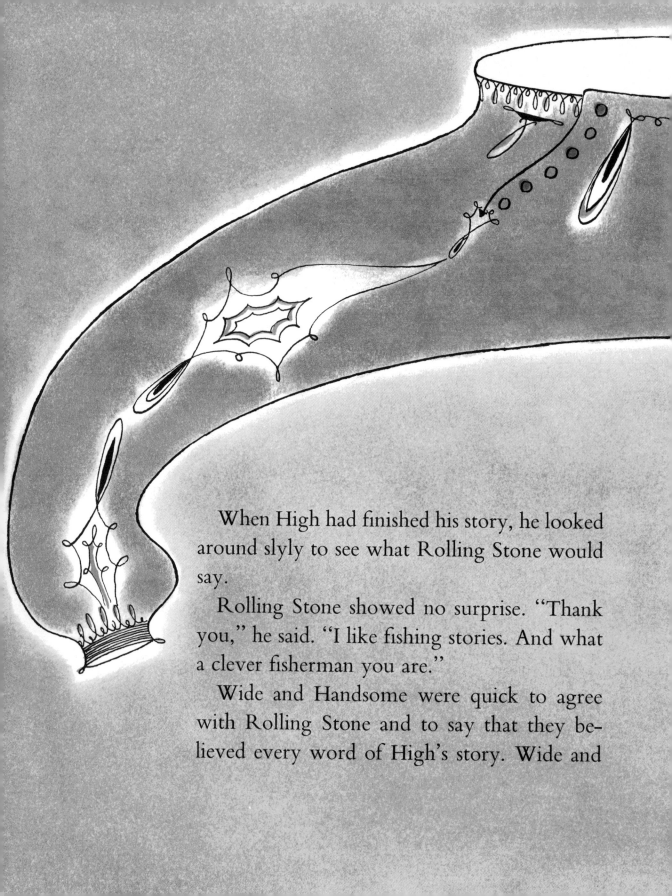

When High had finished his story, he looked around slyly to see what Rolling Stone would say.

Rolling Stone showed no surprise. "Thank you," he said. "I like fishing stories. And what a clever fisherman you are."

Wide and Handsome were quick to agree with Rolling Stone and to say that they believed every word of High's story. Wide and

Handsome were secretly glad High had not
been the one to win Rolling Stone's clothes.

"Now I shall tell a story," said Wide.

Wide could hardly wait to see himself in
Rolling Stone's brocaded trousers, though he
did wonder whether the trousers might not be
a little tight for him.

They could be stretched, he decided. And he
began to tell his story:

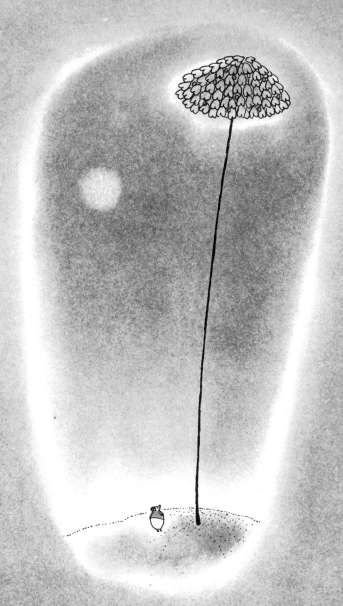

Wide's Story

"Before I was born," said Wide, "I put on my best trousers and went for a walk in the woods. I came upon a tamarind tree a thousand feet high.

"The ripe tamarinds looked delicious. So I climbed the tree and ate until I was full. By then I was so heavy and sleepy that I could not climb down.

"Naturally, I was terribly afraid that I
would fall out of the tree and hurt my-
self. So I ran back to the village and got
a ladder.

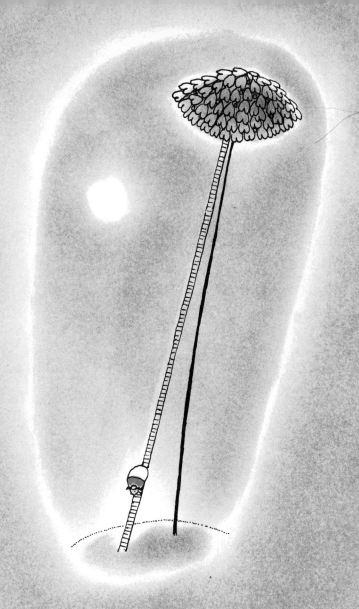

"Then I propped the ladder against
the tree and climbed safely down."

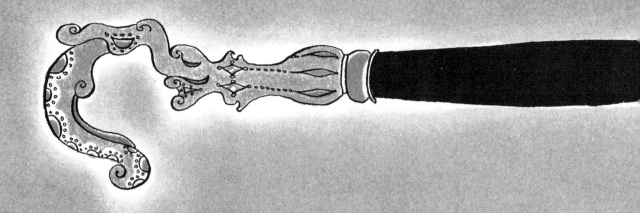

Wide nearly burst out laughing at his own story, and he looked at Rolling Stone, expecting the hound to say, "I don't believe it!"

But Rolling Stone showed no surprise. "You were clever to think of a ladder," he said. "Or you might still be up in the tamarind tree."

High and Handsome, of course, said they believed Wide's story, too. Then it was Handsome's turn to tell a story.

Handsome was glad that High and Wide

had not been able to trick Rolling Stone. He wanted to be the one to take Rolling Stone by surprise.

Handsome could see himself flashing the jeweled walking stick. And he could imagine himself waving the feathered hat to an admiring crowd, which was begging to hear one of his wonderful stories.

Handsome preened his whiskers and began his story:

Handsome's Story

"When I was only a year old," said Handsome, "I was chasing a rabbit. The rabbit ran into a thicket, and I ran after it.

"But as I was about to pounce, the rabbit turned into a tiger. It was the biggest tiger I had ever seen.

"The tiger roared and opened his mouth to swallow me. I objected, of course. I told him that it would be quite unfair of him to eat me, as I had been looking for a rabbit, not a tiger.

"But the tiger paid no attention. As he came toward me, I caught hold of his jaw and gave it a jerk. To my surprise, the tiger broke in two and died."

Handsome finished his story with a perfectly straight face, and looked up at Rolling Stone expectantly.

But Rolling Stone did not look surprised at all. "That poor tiger," he said. "What a clever hunter you are."

High and Wide nodded that they, too, believed Handsome's story. Then it was Rolling Stone's turn.

"I don't know many stories," Rolling Stone said. "While you fellows have been hunting and fishing and eating tamarinds, I have been working at one job or another.

"However," he said, "here is a story that you may find hard to believe."

Rolling Stone cleared his throat and began to tell his story:

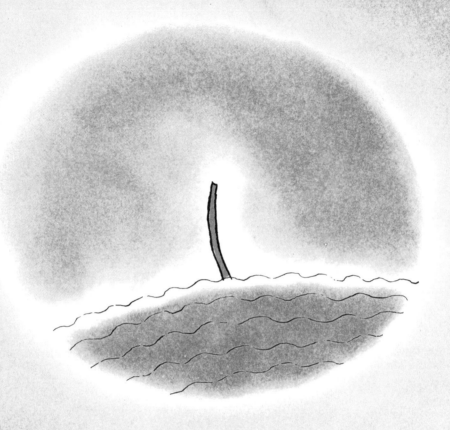

Rolling Stone's Story

"Some years ago," said Rolling Stone, "I bought a coconut farm, and on this farm grew a very strange coconut tree. It was of a bright red color and grew no

higher than a bush. For a long time this
tree had no branches and no leaves.

"One day I decided to chop it down.
But just as I lifted my ax, three branches
suddenly appeared. The branches had
no leaves, but there was a coconut on
each branch.

"I was about to pick the coconuts, when they burst open, and a pig jumped out of one, a fox from the second, and a monkey from the third.

"As the pig and the fox and the monkey came from my coconuts, they were
legally my slaves, and I made them
work on my farm.

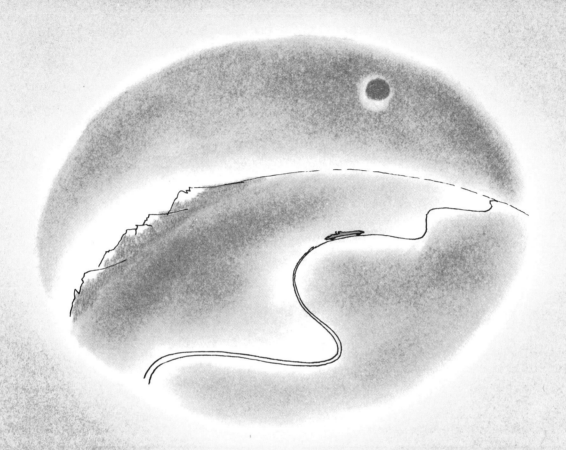

"But being lazy fellows, they ran away, and I have been traveling all over the world looking for them ever since.

"Now, at last, I have found them. My dear fellows, you know very well that you are my runaway slaves, and you must pack at once and come back to my farm with me."

High, Wide and Handsome looked at each
other in astonishment. If they said that they
believed Rolling Stone's story, they would be
agreeing that they were his slaves—and they
would have to do anything that he wished
them to do.

But if they said they *didn't* believe his story,
he would win the bet—and they would *become*
his slaves.

"Speak up," said Rolling Stone. "Do you
believe my story—or don't you?"

High, Wide and Handsome did not know
what to say.

"Very well," laughed Rolling Stone. "No
matter how you answer, I win! Therefore,
you are my slaves and must do whatever I
order you to do."

Then Rolling Stone waved his walking stick
and said, "I order you to give me the clothes
that you are wearing. Take them off, fold them
neatly, and put them in my car."

High, Wide and Handsome had no choice.
They took off their clothes and put them in
Rolling Stone's car.

"And now," said Rolling Stone, "I shall
grant you your freedom. For I am going to
give up farming."

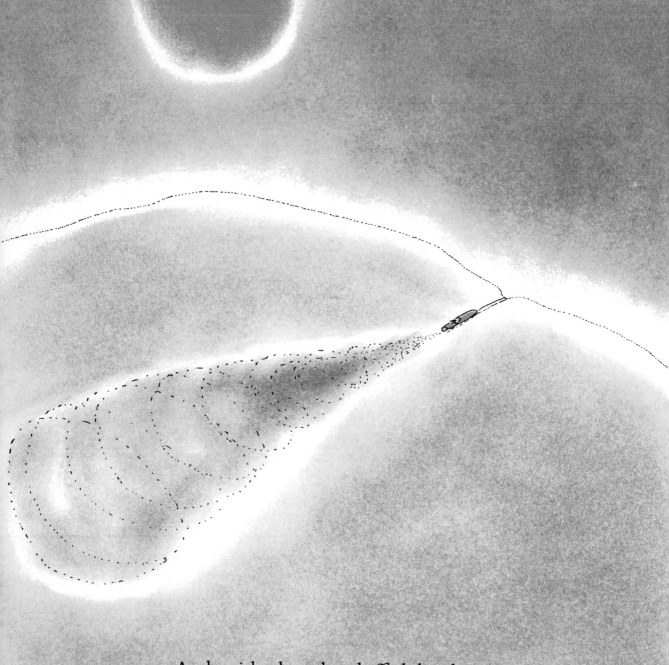

And with that, he doffed his hat, jumped into his car, and disappeared in a cloud of dust.